Visit the author, Antwel T. Higgins, here:
www.instagram.com/antwel.higgins/

Cover illustration by Luis Méndez Rock, visit him here:
www.madriphur.org

Reflective Mirrors

Noah Cohen

'Reflective mirrors, form me a shell
to hide me away from outside hells;
form me an egg to hibernate,
so that I might in peace respirate;
hide me away inside yourself,
inside your protective mirror-shells.'

Contents:

Antael

Vistas, Unchartered

Oceans beneath your eyes

it comes with your soul

with the territory you're given

a glimpse deep down inside

where the rivers converge

where it is you forever live

forever in your eyes

Deep vistas of pain

sorrow and regret

are but patterns to the curtain

the fabric un-torn

ache all you have

Never will it be removed

that depth I see in you

So sail across the sea

come with me, journey, into the deep

breathe, breathe the air, freely

Soul Retrograde

One day when all things seem dead

you will come to see the things I dread

the way it reeks out on the surface

the way you're all led

blind, already dead.

One day when all things come undone!

may you see there was no dread,

no hordes of dead,

may you see that you've been fed

lies and secrets

of a liar's truth, *YOUR DEATH.*

Fed, like stock kept alive, fed

like chickens, led, blind, penned;

no hordes of dead.

Hard, Unyielding Rocks

Hard, unyielding rocks
were as the sand beneath her feet,
carried from youth by the currents
of her age,
until, one day, came a new bent,
along a new page,
moulded and turned by fingers still yet soft,
spoken aloud with lips that broke
the hardest words to fragments
of a wearable, daytime cloth

And from out the mews of sullen
revelry, she began to feel the breeze
of nights' long end come aloft
many strings of softly spoken
favour from youthful saviour's strangely
ageing behaviour

The hard, unyielding rocks
beneath her feet grew still
in pain and felt
far, far away, her home's shore
growing dim,
growing lost, her eyes could but
feel to see only those distant

sands
of renewing, lasting, promised soft
rock where to sail and sink her feet.

The Mysterious Living Thing

There was a thing behind the earth, a thing that lived, a thing that need not breathe. It was a thing quite like no other. It was alive; it wasn't dead.

Eons have passed, they said, and that's how it come to be: a mass of life reaching forthwith to thee; tentacles, singular in their sleep, triangular in it's wake. They longed to live to never die. Peace was to them a tide, distance ever-the-measure. But then came the day, the day in which no one would ever remember.

Two explorers found, stumbling, on clumsy feet, with numb hands and frightfully cold fingers, the most magnificent, most high, in a dark, dark forgotten retreat of caves and holes that led the adventurers to the peak of this creature's hidden keep.

The first Explorer turned to the second, "Astonishing," said the Explorer, but the second did not reply. The second Explorer, though one could not see, the second Explorer's mind, well, it had began to *bleed*. This bleeding was no trick, however, of The Mysterious Living Thing behind the earth. It was a trick of the explorer it had seen; and belonging only to the second Explorer. The Explorer's eyes then, forthwith through vision's deceit, began to undo the tiresome spells of a concrete, unnatural life of which the Explorer had wandered quietly and serene. The Explorer's brain began to itch, lies of his humble grandeur quickly unfold, heart burn; mind bleed.

The first Explorer now found himself helping a friend.

The second Explorer had fallen down, eyes crying, mouth moaning; growing hot very quick, beginning to twitch, tear at one's skin, pull at one's eyes, try to reveal the singular thing which lay within. The first Explorer dropped to his knees, despite all violence of the second, to help the second Explorer, but there was no use.

The second Explorer died.

There is something living behind the earth, which lives and needs not breathe. It is quite like no other:
it is alive, it is not dead.

Revelry of the Mad Cats

'Glory to the world,
the world is dead.'

In the deep dark forest of a jungle, light climbs a grey sky to bring out giant shadows that know only too well how to hide. Dawn is breaking, and one creature, confused among a throng, rushes along a paved sidewalk fraught with the clambering, the bustling, the to and thro, of many rushing creatures alike.

Separating the paved walks of our jungle swims a river, treacherously. Creatures ride one way in this river—back to the depths of the jungle, to where the sea resides; gigantic, hard, metallic and spewing toxic fumes, these are the creatures in the strait (not creatures like a creature on the paths, or any creature,—feral, tamed or otherwise), and these creatures haven't life!

On either side of our little, lost friend, with one close to his right, the other across the strait, flock large and mountainous cliffs of a smooth, refined and dreadful face, black and grey and silver the granite. These are flanking, grand monuments, sentinel to all that transpires, that no creature with life, or mind, durst look up. Our lost, little friend, amongst all other creatures to his like, rushes forward in the only direction he sees.

In the deep dark forest as morning rises and shadows lurk our friend feels quite peculiar and lost, friendless among the creature-folk of his kind. Each day is a haze and every memory like a blur. All he does is walk, work, feel and fear; walk, work, feel, fear. All he does is think. All he can see is madness, unkindness, a rigidity. All he knows is this haze.

Through the haze he plods, as each day and every morn; sunlight lapsing across his back, warmly, the clothes he wears will soon make him sweat. He wonders, Why do we have to wear these suits they dress. He wonders, Why no one talks. No one dares glance. And when nighttime comes, Why tensions aren't revealed, he wonders; Why order breaks free; his peers, creatures alike, they all grunt and laugh, poke and pull, jump and hit. Why does tension rise in the gut at mere thought, he wonders, and shakes it off, and is done.

He wears his suit all night long, whilst the others do not. He hides in waiting for morning to come, whilst the others do not. And when it does, when morning comes, he finds himself here, everyone else, too, and suited, walking forward through the haze, forward into the breaking of dawn.

He looks around, he finds it hard. His neck is stiff. He carries a case in one of his hands, a briefcase he's before never opened, a case he can only recognise with worry and fear. Ahead of him now, he sees his fate. And for the first time in all his memories, he drops the briefcase.

Animals screech as they approach the scene ahead. The haze, it shifts, it tries to invoke his mind and heart. He feels its stroke, its delirious terrible claws under his furry skin, up and down the cavity of his chest, knocking at the ribs of his heart, and they quiver and aren't let in. The creatures before him struggle and fidget. Grunts rise high into the morn and the horde but walks on. The beasts, the metallic-things, the creatures of the river, slither down the strait; their job hard, their job metallic, with black eyes they never gaze back, or side from side, and even their speed is toxic to our friend,—angry, unreliable, way too quick. Thumbs of black air spiral his feet, darkening our little friend's tip-toeing steps as he moves and creeps along the path of hurried bustling.

He sees it then!, with clarity, the terror, the windless, hollow defeat. Through a black archway, in the cliff face jutting out ahead, an archway, quite like a mouth, terrible and waiting to feed. He sees the animals stumbling through, and then jagged teeth, like large shutters, snapping, shut then open, shut then open. He remembers what happens when one fidgets through these doors. He has seen it himself, almost encountered it. Limbs, arms, legs, feet, once a head, twice a torso, cut in two, splashes of blood for proof, steep slopes each a side their fate.

We venture through. Stiff and still he, silently shrill, his voice dare not raise alarm, even by mental introspect, thoroughly choked. The dark is cold, the sun out from reach. His feet plod along a narrow metal floor—each side a treacherous fall. Walking,—many plummet, many do not—; echoes of noise, screeching, laughing, muttering, feet come scurrying, shuffle shuffle. He finds his way, straight along, across the narrow, metal corridor that seems so, ever-so-long!

At the end, and defined by light, he sees things that confuse his mind of what is right. The walls are red to one his sides. Shadows move quick off the walls, strike what they hold in black-dark hands—animals that panicked, who chose to turn, scramble, ran. They grab then strike with cleavers twice, the red on walls their proof of might, of death, of limbs decapitated and creatures dropped into the pit, into the pit.

On walks our friend, not calm, but straight. His suit dripping with sweat. His limbs, feverish, feel the need to take his leave, but he listens not. To his left is blinding lights. He does not look, turn to see; for he has done so and he knows what's there, left and right; left: your eyes hurt, the blinding lights; your steps might sway! Right: you see the shadows whom take those that ran, you see their limbs fallen into buckets filled and spilling; and that terrible wall aback the scene covered in a thick, red slime—the blood of retreat.

A hand brushes his shoulder from the right. He does not quiver, does not take flight. Instead, he walks on, stiff and still, not calm, but straight. He won't be chopped; he won't be dead before the night; he will survive, for to him it is right.

Through a door of blinding lights he staggers from the darkness and the horrors left behind. Hands grab his shoulders. He's hurried along, pushed down a path that feels slippery, and familiar, and feels right. The hands disappear, and all around becomes filled with momentary cheer. Then the darkness grows still.

From behind, left and right, from in front, all around, he feels bodies stumble and cry. They are all waiting, queueing in hordes for the next ride, the dark their bride…. Eventually then, after and through plenty of shuffling, bumping, budging, fidgeting, wriggling, struggling, our little friend falls forward, stumbles, collapses, then stands upright in a cold, hard-casing.

A roaring beast he finds himself inside, quivering. The door he came by closes. The beast roars, rumbles, moves. As its speed grows forward and forward it rocks from side to side and something happens for the very first time: a glass smashes to his left and on his right: light for the first time shoots into the belly he resides.

The dark gone, the beast rocks violently from side to side, side to side, and eventually, our friend finds himself looking outside, and he sees the hordes walking by the strait, the cliffs' faces of cold and hard, smooth granite stone staring.—And he sees, up high, the naked creatures, peering down, on ridges, what otherwise would have gone unseen. They all wear hats, tall hats, and they laugh and laugh, their bellies bloated, their eyes full and aglow, with soft gentle light. They laugh and laugh, our friend hears them through the haze in glimpsing, but then, the Mad Cats, they're gone from his sight. Sped away, the sea yet a journey, our little friend feels the Revelry spent.

You Killed You

Your death will be murder,
Your life smoke,
And your body shall smoulder in the ruins you'll choke

I was your friend in the beginning: your social partner,
your best buddy, your warm relief. I was your ticket to
the world. Hell, you abused me, took me for granted.
Then the *happiness* burnt away. Didn't it.

Our love turned to ash, spreading, intoxicating your
every cell; you turned, mutating before me, falling to
scold me with your cancerous hate.

But, it was *your* fault in the end. *Your* fault. *You* killed
you. Not I.

Your grip slackened on me as the days grew old and
your life's end loomed in full surety. Nevertheless, our
love stayed stubborn, like an irrevocable stain. You
couldn't push me away. You couldn't merely even try, as
I had weakened your soul; for my suffocating, toxic
demand had thrived, always, always to be your bane—
and you let it!

I wouldn't let you go. YOU wouldn't let me go.

17

Do you still blame me? Well, don't. It was you. You all along! Though I know you can't hear me, you *never* could, I'm still here. I'm with you now. YES, even as you struggle to draw breath, I poison your every cell, staining your very life with my chemical siege.

It's too late now. For I did my work. I poisoned your being, your life, your health, your thoughts, your heart, your lungs. I poisoned you.

If only you'd have listened to your family or friends. Maybe then, maybe, you wouldn't be here, laying on this hospital bed, dying and laying as all those caring for you stare down upon what is to be left. And I stare down too, you know. YES, I stare up with you and down with them; for *you* have brought me into *their* lives now.

Yes. Yes. They will be *mine* soon. One day soon. For as long as they breathe my travelling poisons, my inescapable poison, or the poison you share with your decaying life, your forgotten and intoxicating failure of a being too simple to even *see!* the poison of sadness and despair that I through you have cast upon thee, YES. Their happy little lives will be mine now.

Soon, soon, soon soon, you will be gone, every happiness you ever had, gone. All the memories you have, memories of your children, your own parents, of Christmases spent with family, laughs and tears shared with friends, lovers, people you all cared for. Gone.

Gone to the world as your brain, your life, decays within you, *here* on this hospital bed.

HAHAHAHA-HAHAHAHA-hahaha.

Happiness. Happiness. Oh, that word. That feeling. How empty does it feel now? As small and insignificant as a grain of sand on a beach you once visited? For that is the fate of you, your petty joys, your family's memory of you, as all shall be rememberable of such being who dies to insignificance, living so *insignificant*, remembered as such, as a single grain of that sand on which a million faded lives have walked, all gone to the decaying wind of time, a wind you met TOO early, gone and scattered, *wasted*. Oh, your pretty smelling flesh. Scattered to the winds, like dirt, forgotten, paved over and walked on.

Wait, wait, what is that?... is that death? YES! I see the life shrivelling from your eyes. We can all see it: your last breath escaping; your life drifting; and death succeeding, finally, under my poisonous reign.

Your family watch through a scolding blur of tears.

A shell, a corpse, nothing more, nothing more left than a blackness to fill your place.

HA! I'll see you in the dirt, six feet under, where I can taunt YOU *forevermore*!

> *Your death was murder,*
> *Your life is smoke,*

And your body smoulders on the ruins you choked.

But wait ... There's still time ... Today.

Without Wings

He came when I needed him most. The stranger without wings. I haven't for him a name, other than what you will hear me call him by. He saved me, and he's out there now, still; a shade of the night, figure draped in black,—ominous stranger.

This will only be a short entry I am afraid. I have not much to say and the recount is brief at best. So, Dear Diary, will you hear how I was saved tonight?

It is winter and it is cold. The night is drawn across the skies with a heavy darkness, starless-black. The moon has vanished, all trace of its light seemingly absent beneath the stark winter blackness of the late and unfortunate night that I write this upon. I was walking home from work, my heels clicking on the pavement, when they came for me;

unsatisfied customers from the strip-club that I work. Passers by that neither live in this here town or care for its people. They grabbed me and dragged me into a dark corner where no street light shone and no whisper dared escape. They held my mouth. I bit a hand. They hit me hard. My clothes were easy to come off.

Rape the bitch! I heard one of them say. And then it happened. They took me. Four or five of them hoarding around my struggling figure like a rabid pack of horny dogs that would sooner rip out my throat than see me on my way again. My head was slammed hard into the side of a concrete wall. Everything went numb. My ears rung loudly. He put himself inside of me. The first one. And if it wasn't for him, he I haven't yet a name, I doubt I'd be home right now. I doubt I'd have lived to tell you this story, Diary. How they would have left me, I do not know.

The night was dark, cold and unkind. Cruel. Bitterness had made like a fog in the air, and when he came, there was no light that followed him, there were only screams.

The men dropped me, their hands whisked away by something unseen in the dark around. The man atop me vanished, pulled away sharply. He wailed the loudest and I felt myself bleeding. Their screams were petulant and they filled the night air. Though, I do not think he harmed them. I do not know of what he did. He saved my life, and for that I am thankful.

He was a shadow darker than the blackness of all winter nights passed. More evasive than the fog that stung the air with its bitter breeze. He had pulled them all away, and so fast. I don't know where they went but they were gone, they were all gone when next I could stand. I whimpered in the dark and looked around. I felt overhead a soft and gentle breeze rising to the sky above. And I believe I saw him: A pair of eyes staring down, neither kind nor unkind, merely watching me, a white and shimmering golden, tinted with a red haze, and then eyelids, a-fluttering, a dark and fleshy purple blink through the black of night above, and he turned away, and he was gone. And that is all I saw, or, at least, believe that I saw.

I stood up and started for home. I felt so horribly weak and bruised. But I was alive, my assailants gone. And my saviour. I know it sounds all so strange. But I don't think he had wings. He wasn't an angel, or anything bright like that. He wasn't a demon, either. But he saw me through the fog of a dark and despairing night, and he spared my insignificance.

Photosynthesis of Life Drive

the Night is not bright,
it is very Black
of colour
toward the non-presence
of Light;
but the Day is very White
and full
of shinning Light

heat lives hotter
in Days of great
bright
shinning
White
Light

Nights, always colder
after Days long endured
the hotter

Black, it self however, we know
through colour absorbs
White
shinning
bright

Light,
like we know
White
reflects the shining
of the Light

but why, oh
why
is it this balance so,
--maybe so
we do never not die?
maybe
Conscious-ness it self,
of colours,
of Life is
through my, THIS, *The Evolutionary Drive*;

red-rea mine Name, removing thine
Self.

Art of Peace

Art of Peace begins with You; work on self in the Art of Peace; everyone has a Spirit of deep energy they may refine, a body to love, a path to make. Here and there with the Art of Peace may you find Your true self, foster peace, enlighten all around You;--through the passive voice of no words and true wisdom, find and share in the freedom of scrupulous doubt and hate.

Persadonia: Prologue

The personality is a shield. There are philosophers whom say it is a myth, that the personality is not real. But real is to real what real is. And the personality, well, it can be as real as a kick in the teeth, or the allure of the perfumed girl; it is as a shield; an innate reaction, an instinct melded throughout time, life after life; or, those that grow teeth, it is a projection; and those without teeth, too, they project, like I do, they project when they need to, or they look the other way, redirect the inner current, and smile with loving gums. So, after having met so many people, grown to know, grown to trust, grown to love, I simply do not speak anymore. I keep silence and I see you, because I see who you are not.

Lovgic

Love is a fortress

Love is a dome

Love what you can

Love not what you own

Love be your throne

Love a day

Love explain

What to say

Feel

Go

Love be a dome

Love be the place

Where to go

You Rome

You loved to love

Honour and pain

Honour and slaves

Love yourself

Love not your own

Love is ...

Your dome you roam,

Like a fortress you keep,

Enslaved in honour,

Honoured by pain,

Never retreat.

P-rayer

No persons need pray, not, at least, any person that can watch a sunset, or find hope in themselves, an image to climb toward, and strive ever inwardly toward the still and peaceful horizon of the most true and great of their aspirations;--know it ye who would search and look that when the transitioning rays of the sun stroke the sky and paint that far and most high region in colours of fire and gold, there comes a prayer in the eyes of the most true, prayer for greatness, a sense of liberation complete, content, comprehensible only by the silence that has sprung from within.

Amidst Turbulence

Contents:

"Logic isn't *everything*; neither is sight, nor smell; nor sense! The world is *everything*. Isn't it? Nor is it just the question, though. But, the centre?"
-said The 'Angel Without Wings'.

Made for Each Other

I was made for you
and you were made for me,

all by one person,
one being and one thing

all was made for you,
all was made by not me.

When Light Fades

Writing poems late at night,
I feel no delight,

for the light in my heart is
fading fast,

and I want it to always last,

Fragments of a Uniglass

Accept metaphors;
except the logic, access
fragments of a Uniglass.

Points of Stabilisation

My bones feel weak and legs
are heavy,

I'm nearin' the point, I'm
nearing

to stabilise, but I feel it all the
more,

heavy upon me, the weight
from within;

propellers through nights so
dreary,

why it feels I might never
win?

Balance

We are balance. Perspective lines within a system. We are balance. Emotional desires filled with controversy. We are balance; existing on a point that has no end, has no beginning, has only infinity. We are balance. Embrace the phenomenon; balance in the reality.

Peace of Balance

The peace of balance
comes warred upon the
balance
of peace and war.

Sunshine and Darkness

The sun still shines
but all around I'm in darkness.

Like the bottom of a deep,
deep well

I have fallen. I climb and I
climb.

I cannot leave you behind.

You are forever on my mind.

Who we were. Who you that
made me.

I felt free.

Nothing real before could
have ever weighed upon me,

but now, for of you, you who
have made me strong.

I'm sorry. I made some mistake.
But to leave

it behind, now, would be ever
wrong…

Laying in a Shallow Stream

Laying in a shallow stream on his back and with a friend, he asked, "Why do *you think* the water moves around us?" "I don't know," replied his friend.

"Yeah, I guess so."

Laying in the stream, the water continuing to flow around hem, visions of the night sky above became deeper and more black; more diluted with pixels twinkling as stars above, more transparent with less colour etched upon the seams from that of heir world beneath.

"I wonder what makes us move," asked the man in the middle of the swirling stream.

Wilderness and Light

Stay, my friend and not my
fiend

from out the wilderness
where it may seem

less; unsettled and more serene.

Stay, my friend, in the middle
and away from the sea of an
edge
of endless and troublesome dreams.

Stay, my friend and not my fiend,

from out the nether realm
and seams.

Stay, my friend, within the middle.

Stay my friend from the edge of many seams.

Evolving Matrix

Through a riptide of controversy, I align myself
with thoughts gained higher, I reach from out what I am
and to to what I will be. I take life and I become fire. The
wind is my breath, and I breathe you in. The seas are my
tears. The salt is my pain. The skies from within the
quiet, the waves that begin to rest. I am evolving. I am
travelling. I am the matrix, at my best.

Black Holes in Formation

Black Holes are Time Hops
Dimension Drops,
Black Holes are all lights'
Darkest Kites

Hollow yet filled with sight,
of no real, tangible height

Arranged in Time and Space
holes that sit and gape
holes that tear away
the Fabric of Time and Space

Riddles we see in the Light
Truths we know in the Dark

Enough can be *said*
But can it be *done?*

Infinitely capable of harm
Infinitely capable of life

Forever do hope no one learns
Of truths that *WILL* burn
this Earth and all its Sights,

Time, Life, Principles Of Life

Evolution by Light

Look, no more Blaring Lights in the dark of night.
Understand, only Fire as Light is *ever ever* right.

Today, as all days, you read Letters as Words,
information produced, so, please do process my
Electrical Impulses with *your* Brain,

not the other way around,
staring at lights till eyes *burn* in PAIN!

Oh, how I wish there weren't all these Bright, Bright
Lights! on a night.
Oh, how I wish all would have more
Inner Sight!

Vanish!
Be gone

Contents:

"Intelligence is arrogance, emotion is understanding; but that doesn't mean you have to be emotional to be understanding, nor arrogant to be intelligent." - Lu Tien Oloiv

Beneath The Woods of Gsuilamacecmicmisc

The Magic Wood comes alive,
when music chimes deep
In Hives. Their allege seeps and
Toad Stools flutter, Magic
Chimes singing songs of sunder,
when music rings in the
Dead of Night. Stars up high
cry with light, whilst trees beneath
whisper over feet,
leaves and branches,
air, Creatures' swinging feats,
mud and locks of grass and other
things all caught beneath
in the deep of Gsuilamacecmicmisc's

Keep.

Set of Eyes

A contradiction consisting of two
different halves of a biological thing;
a thing of raw material, of pure existence;
physically contradicting. A thing with

two hands. One being large. Almost monstrous.
The other small. Completely deformed,
like that of an unsightly, shrivelled thing.

This creature exists in darkness.
There is no light to bring to this thing
into true creation, instead it sleeps
like a thing hibernating, un-wanting of life

outside of my verse. Its body is contained
within unseen lines of creation, a creature
that is neither alive nor dead.

It is where outside of these matters is a world
you well know, a world constructed
of ideas explained to you.
But with *my* box, I hide in the

darkness, my little friend is
neither alive nor dead,
neither real nor not,
My little friend, he exists inside my head;

A place that I can choose whether
or not I listen to what the world might
have said; a place where I can hide my true

set of eyes.

Beast of the Blue Moon

Before darkness shall come an after-light
skyline drawn across the horizon like
the colour of an old, purple bruise
beneath that of the greyish-blue-sky of the afternoon;
as the moon hangs in the blue and yawns
of the latening hour that will soon
beset the skyline like a deathly streak
darkening the stratosphere and condemning all to fear
of a fate beneath the earth, encrusted
in a blaze of death and insanity and the crushing
soul-fracturing stare of the most hurt and pained;
for it is believed that the End's Beast
shall come in the colour of night,
and he will set terror upon the lands
in legions of darkness from Devil-worshiping slums;
the night sky will finally collapse around the moon,
causing utter darkness but for the one distant light, like a
gloom
from beneath the bottom of a hazy swamp, watching
with a glowing eye the world in wake of Death's
impaling;
watching as the lands burn beneath dark skies of the
Beast's incantation.

The Boogie Man

Walking down the road, he smiles
when he passes.
Crossing a road you might recognise
Him.
Neighbour, friend, or family
member you hardly ever knew
You'll pass him on the street and
He won't catch your eye.
He once lived next door to you,
but he doesn't
anymore.
Somewhere, in the dark,
throughout time immemorial, you will bump into that
fiend
you hardly knew. And then, my friend,
you might want to hear
that it can be seen in his eyes
first; the darkness that will arise,
and shadows descend.
Then shaking your hand
In the middle of some stairwell,
The man you shall see shall be of the man
I speak. A dark man we all keep.

Six will reveal
my permanent eclipse.

Truly Poetry

We write poems to express,
and we express what we feel,

our thoughts; all being constructed
of a world we learnt; we are taught;

but what of this statement is in reality living?
—Good poetry should come from within,

as it is within that we are;
and so, poetry, should, to your subconscious, be true;

and, since, poetry in itself is used to show
what we cannot without a straightly constructed road,

is it not within where you truly
find the reflection to questions left unanswered?

Contained Reflect

Like a flame in the dark, your life exists;
like the flickering leaves atop tall trees;
like dense, dark air of some deep-forest mist;
like a caged bird with a mirror to see;
your life exists as though of great choice;
of a choice you'd believe yourself not unfree;
but in truth, outside your bars, something waits; frozen
ice;
for the cold that you walk, of your life's bare stage;
gifted with choice and plagued with stark chains;
where darkness surrounds, you flicker in a wind;
for your world's so dark, even light commands sin;
and when thoughts are stable, your mind be unhinged.

Like a flame in the dark, your life exists;
like dense, dark air of some deep-forest mist.

Thinking of You

My heart was strong, my words true,
When love through my lips spoke to you.
And even now, when you are gone,
My heart stays true, my words are strong.

No pain will weigh too much upon my shoulder.
No challenge, no burden, too much for me
to carry. For my heart stays true, grows bolder
all for you; from anguish to strength, I am freed;

yours from afar, yours through and through.
For as much as I have by this pain been prolonged,
as much as I have wished, sourly, for another earth,

I have stayed so I may right all of my wrongs.

Even as you read this now, when I think of you,
my heart beats strong, and my words ever true.

Colourful Anger

A colourless Man's conscience
can be swept away from foulness,
like a dirty floor cloth discards of

muck. A white Man's conscience
smells of that of a scent dictated by
an old power; for once where they

might have stood and been able, they now
are not. Yet even so, they sink lower, still,
than our wits ever 'had', by smearing

our freedom with dirt—like a mucky
cloth is used to upon dirty floor.

One day, may *you* know how it was.

Restless in Darkness

Atop a hill speckled
in a bright sunlight gold,
I sit surrounded by beneath
a forest of sinister retreat
where darkness comes to lay wake
and nothing dare sleep for the crawling of black walls;
tho I sit fearlessly above,
the forest beneath,
atop a hill speckled
in a blinding sunlight gold,
I write of the creeps that slither
beneath the clustered skies of all restless sleep.

Blue in Seas

Falling Skies bleed a red
Glowing Clouds spur away

Nights' sure fall
over blueless seas

Darkness' reigns
but the Dead of Night

then Mornings' come
and skies will bleed

their colour red
over Blue in Seas

'End'

<u>About the author</u>

Antwel T. Higgins hails from West Yorkshire, where he lives quite happily with his mother and two dogs. His genres are Cosmic-Horror and Cosmic-Fantasy. He studied Literature and Creative Writing at university in York. His pseudonym is an anagram;—can you figure it out? _ _ _ _ _ _ _ _ _ _ _ _ _ _ _ _ _ _ _ _